A NOVEL

# Fox Magic

A NOVEL

# Fox Magic

## BEVERLEY BRENNA

Red Deer Press

Published in Canada by Red Deer Press
195 Allstate Parkway, Markham, ON  L3R 4T8

Published in the United States by Red Deer Press
311 Washington Street, Brighton, MA  02135

10 9 8 7 6 5 4 3 2 1
Red Deer Press acknowledges with thanks the Canada Council for the Arts and the Ontario Arts Council for their support of our publishing program. We acknowledge the financial support of the Government of Canada through the Canada Book Fund (CBF) for our publishing activities.

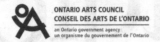

ONTARIO ARTS COUNCIL
CONSEIL DES ARTS DE L'ONTARIO
an Ontario government agency
un organisme du gouvernement de l'Ontario

Canada Council    Conseil des arts
for the Arts      du Canada

Library and Archives Canada Cataloguing in Publication
Brenna, Beverley A., author
Fox magic / Beverley Brenna ; illustrations by Miriam Körner.

ISBN 978-0-88995-552-3 (softcover)

I. Körner, Miriam, 1975-, illustrator  II. Title.

PS8553.R382F69 2017        jC813'.54        C2017-904102-9

Publisher Cataloging-in-Publication Data (U.S.)

Names: Brenna, Beverley, 1962-, author. | Körner, Miriam, 1975-, illustrator.
Title: Fox magic / Beverley Brenna ; illustrations by Miriam Körner.
Description: Markham, Ontario : Red Deer Press, 2017. |Summary: "A twelve-year-old girl in a small town must overcome loss to suicide and face bullying. This story of hope includes a mysterious magical fox that helps her find courage in the power of dreams. The book includes resources for dealing with grief, loss and suicide" – Provided by publisher.
Identifiers: ISBN 978-0-88995-552-3 (pbk.)
Subjects: LCSH: Grief—Juvenile fiction. | Suicide – Juvenile fiction. | Bildungsromans. | BISAC: YOUNG ADULT FICTION / Coming of Age.
Classification: LCC PZ7.B746Fo |DDC [F] – dc23

Edited for the Press by Peter Carver
Text and cover design by Tanya Montini

Cover image by GDallimore used under Creative Commons, GNU Free Documentation License, Attribution-ShareAlike 3.0 Unported

Printed in Canada

*To our children*

# Chapter One

The week after the Bad Thing happened, Chance is back in school. She's walking away from the water fountain and Monika is right there in front of her.

"She was my cousin, you know," Monika hisses. "It should have been you."

Chance just shakes her head and tries to get by.

"Both of them were better than you," Monika says.

Chance stands still, head down. Nobody else was supposed to know about the suicide pact. Does Monika know? What about the other kids? She waits until Monika turns into the classroom. Then she follows. There is nowhere else to go. At least, not right now.

Beverley Brenna

# Chapter Two

When Chance wakes up, her mouth is dry and her heart is pounding. "Breathe!" she tells herself. "Just breathe." It takes a moment to realize that she's in her room with music playing from her alarm.

*Breathing in. Breathing out.* She says the words in her head the way she and her counselor have practiced. When her pulse stops racing, she reaches over and bangs the clock radio until it's silent.

It's Monday morning. The start of a new week. Or simply a copy of last week, and the week before *that*, and the week before that. The week before that was when the Bad Thing happened, almost a month ago now, but Chance doesn't want to remember. It feels as if the memory of the Bad Thing is padding around her bed like a wildcat, ready to pounce. And Chance hates cats. She always has.

She throws back the covers, sits up, and leans toward the window, pushing aside the curtain. It's a new flowered curtain that her mother's sewn to replace the old blinds, and it runs easily on its hooks—no strings.

Outside, the sun is hesitating on the horizon. A new day. Or is it just a duplicate day in a long straight line of days, standing like dominoes, waiting until one of them falls and knocks down the others?

Everything out there is gray. Gray sky. Gray trees. The matted leaves are like a drab quilt with dead grass poking through. For a moment, Chance thinks she sees a flicker of red-gold weaving among the bushes at the edge of the yard, something solid and oddly familiar, but, as she stares, she realizes that she's mistaken. Nothing out there is alive except the wind. It's only the ninth of October, but Chance can feel wintry air pressing through cracks around the window frame. Even the wind feels gray.

The Bad Thing paws at her memory, trying to get a foothold. She looks back at the clock, feeling desperate. Already eight-thirty. How has half an hour passed while she's been staring at the yard? There's still time to pull on her clothes, grab a bowl of cereal, and hustle the few blocks to school before the nine o'clock bell. But she doesn't want to. Something in her, some engine, won't start. She lets gravity pull her back under the covers, rolling onto her right side with only the deaf ear open to the world. Then she squeezes her eyes shut, gratefully letting herself drift away from everything.

At noon, when the phone rings, Chance knows she should get up to answer it, but she doesn't move. Lying on her back, her arms and legs are totally relaxed. At the end of each day, they feel as stiff as the bolts on an old car. She stretches her feet into the cool places on the soft sheets and then pulls them back into warmth.

Ten rings. Eleven. Twelve. The ringing stops. She imagines herself as Georgia's Ford Mustang, the car they'd been fixing with Desiree just before the Bad Thing happened. Just like the car, deserted now in Auntie's garage, she feels deserted, too. Her mom and dad at work. Her grandparents gone to Arizona for the winter. And her friends ...

The phone rings again. It's probably the school, calling a second time. Or her mom. She rolls over onto her right side so that she can't hear it.

Her mother is standing beside the bed wearing her blue nursing scrubs. She doesn't look happy.

"Chance, I can't be coming home every day to get you up for school! And neither can Dad. Not unless he books another leave of absence. You know we work shifts, and the doctors and our patients need us. Come on, you've got to be more responsible!"

"I don't feel good. I think I have a sore throat."

"You're fine! No excuses. Get up out of that bed and you can grab a granola bar on the way out. I'll drive you."

"I don't feel good!" Chance turns her good ear away from her mother, preferring to scramble her mother's orders if she can. But the words break through.

"It's only for the afternoon, and then if you're still complaining, we can go to the clinic after supper. And then—"

"Can't I just stay home today?" Chance interrupts.

"Nope. You've had too many days at home, and Grade 7 is important. Come on. Which top do you want to wear?"

Chance grabs the closest one, a black sweatshirt. She feels like one of those dominoes, dark and dangerous. If she falls, she'll knock down everyone near her. She knows that for a fact. But that's their problem. Isn't it? And anyway, they can get up again. Isn't it better to be in control, take charge of whatever's going to happen? Even if it means the end? Better than waiting for trouble.

"I wouldn't miss anything," she mutters.

"What?" asks her mother, turning around, the car keys in her hand. "What, Chance?"

"Nothing," Chance says, and follows her mom out to the car. She has to be careful. Her parents can't know what she's thinking. Anyway, a couple more hours and she can be home again. Back in bed. That's the only place where the Bad Thing can't reach, try as it might. Out here, in the middle of town, it can easily get at her.

"Why aren't you wearing that blue jacket of yours?" her mom asks when Chance slips into the front seat beside her. "It's cold."

"I don't know. Maybe I lost it," Chance mumbles. Her mother sighs.

"It's important you take care of yourself. And stick to regular routines," her mother says finally, pulling a Kleenex from the box between the seats and pressing it into Chance's hand. "You were doing so well last week. Now, wipe those tears and remember to ask about your homework. We can't have you falling behind. Come on, Chance—you can do it!"

*I can't*, Chance thinks, blowing her nose and then taking another Kleenex as more tears fill her eyes.

"We go back to Dr. Hansen on Thursday. And we can see if she'll offer anything else for these blues," says her mom. "But for now, the best thing—the very best thing—is to keep going. One foot after the other. Okay?"

"Yeah," says Chance, forcing herself from the car and into the parking lot. She knows her mother will wait until she gets inside the school, and she drags her feet, moving as slowly as possible.

"And look for that jacket!" her mother calls out.

The afternoon bell has already gone. Now she'll need to stop at the front desk for a late slip. And when she enters the classroom, everyone will stare.

*Her two best friends killed themselves*. There she is. Just standing there.

"For now," Chance mutters as she flings open the door of the school. "Just for now."

Beverley Brenna

# Chapter Three

Chance is answering in monosyllables, because that will make the appointment with the doctor go more quickly.

"Yes," she wants to feel better.

"No," she isn't trying to get anybody's attention by moping around.

"Yes," she can think clearly and make decisions.

"Yes," she's eating normally and getting enough sleep.

"She might be getting too much sleep," her mother interrupts from the other side of the appointment room. "And she's not eating so well when she's sleeping all the time."

"Sometimes it's hard to sleep at night, so I want to sleep in," Chance mutters.

"Have you read those resources I sent home with you last time?" asks the doctor. "Checked out any of the online sites?"

"No," says Chance. "I mean, yes. Everything's fine. I'm fine."

"And you would tell me if you weren't feeling fine?"

"Uh huh," says Chance.

"And you still don't want to explore any options about that left ear? You know the good thing about having all this medical attention is that sometimes opportunities you didn't know existed can be explored."

"What?" says Chance.

"Your ear. You don't want us to try and help you with that?"

"What?" Chance repeats.

"Very funny," says the doctor.

"I can hear fine. If I want to," Chance says.

"And there's nothing new that you want to tell me? About anything?"

Chance shakes her head.

Her mother interrupts again.

"She just got a math test back. A hundred percent. So that's a good sign!"

"Yes, that's a very good sign," says the doctor. "Shows that you're concentrating on the present, just as you should. Good for you, Chance! Keep it up, and things will start feeling more normal soon."

*Normal?* thinks Chance, turning her good ear away from them. *Like soon it'll be Desiree's birthday and we'll have a junk-food party, like always?* But she doesn't say it. She also doesn't say anything about school that day, about the notes shoved into her desk, about the way the other kids keep their distance. Because that's nothing new.

"Good riddance to bad rubbish," she muttered when she saw that the others in her group had eased their desks away from hers.

The image of dominoes flies back into her mind. One domino falling against another falling against another. Except, in her case, the first domino stayed upright while the other two tumbled down. Desiree and Georgia had gone through with it. But at the last minute, Chance had chickened out. Something she can never tell her parents. She can never tell anyone that she was part of it.

Everybody knows she and Desiree and Georgia were best friends. Whatever Monika's heard, it could be just rumors. It's not a stretch to imagine Chance could be involved in what happened. She's trying hard to forget, though. Trying hard to pretend she wasn't there at all. But the memory of her broken promise is around every corner, behind every door. Waiting. Waiting for her like the worst thing in the world.

After school on Friday, Chance takes the long way home, past Georgia's place. The lights are all off. Auntie Verdine isn't home. Chance stands at the edge of the lawn for a moment, staring at the garage where Auntie had set them up with the car. When

Chance unlocks the garage door, she's hit immediately by the dusty perfume of mice. She carefully checks the traps. Nothing. And all the cheese is gone. Now she'll have to try peanut butter. If she's going to keep working on the car, that is. She looks at it, unsure.

The old blue 1996 Mustang was a gift to Georgia for her tenth birthday. It had needed work, but they figured that by the time they had their driver's licenses, the car would at least be roadworthy.

"It was my best car," Auntie told them, over and over. "And I'm gonna enjoy riding around in it when you guys drive me places."

Auntie couldn't drive anymore because of her diabetes. It had started to affect her eyes and, when the doctor told her that driving would be dangerous, Georgia said Auntie cried for a long time. But when she gave Georgia the car, Auntie was happy again.

"I'm gonna keep my window down and make sure everybody sees how much I'm enjoying the ride!" Auntie said, each time she brought them snacks like carrots and celery sticks. "I'm gonna love it!"

Over the past two years, they'd gotten various tools that were now an undeniable set: an adjustable wrench, a torque wrench, a socket and ratchet set, pliers, Phillips and flathead screwdrivers, and a new hydraulic jack, because the old bumper jack that came with the car hadn't been safe.

At the beginning of summer holidays, they'd scraped together enough money for the right kind of protective mask, and then taken turns using it in a series of assaults on the front brake pads until they finally had them changed. What use had it been, when they'd never drive the car anyway?

Now the tools lie on the floor of the garage like dead bodies, legs splayed, arms out. A Mars Bar wrapper is crumpled beside one of the screwdrivers. A reminder of Georgia's sweet tooth. Desiree preferred salt—chips, pretzels, Cheezies. And Chance went along with both of them—happy to snack on whatever was at hand.

But that was then. Now the thought of food makes her stomach sick. The doctor finally told her parents to let her alone, said she'd eat when she was ready. But she isn't ready yet. Even though she's wearing new jeans, two sizes smaller than her old ones.

The next job on the Mustang is spark plugs, last in the list of things Desiree had written in the folder under *Stuff To Fix*. Chance looks at the folder. She doesn't want to touch it, doesn't want to flip through to find the instructions for *spark plugs*.

But her hands reach out, brush off the dust, open the folder. She reads the journal that Georgia kept in the front, listing their completed work. Completed before. Before they'd come to the conclusion that life in this town was impossible. Before they'd made the plan. The plan that finished with the Bad Thing.

Chance throws down the folder and sees the two bags of dominoes sitting there on the shelf. She takes one domino from each bag and tucks them into her pocket. Then she backs away from the shelf and walks away from the car, away from the garage, and then runs the short distance home as if something is chasing her. Which it is.

When she gets to her bedroom, her arms and legs are aching. She empties her backpack, carefully piling the handful of notes in the top drawer of her dresser with the others. Reading them first, of course.

Somehow the more she reads, the more she feels she deserves them, no matter how awful they are. Then she sees the new notebook and pen the counselor has given her, remembering Mrs. Morin's instructions to keep a journal of her thoughts. But instead she wipes her eyes and crawls under the covers. Tired. She is so tired.

The first thing Chance thinks about when she wakes up on Monday is that today is Desiree's twelfth birthday. Last year, she and Georgia bought all of Desiree's favorite foods and they stayed up all night at Desiree's house watching old Harry Potter movies. Cheezies. Popcorn. Chips and dip, and salty chocolate. The works!

Probably they'd be celebrating tonight if the Bad Thing hadn't happened. But it did happen. As it pushes itself into

Chance's mind, everything else goes into hiding. She turns her head and sees through the gap in her curtains that the sky is gray. And inside her, grayness purrs its satisfaction, stretching into her chest and throat, claws coming out. Then the pain is unbearable. She can't stand it. The Bad Thing has her and it isn't letting go.

"Chance!" calls her father from the kitchen. "Breakfast!"

The Bad Thing vanishes at the sound of Dad's voice, but Chance knows it's only a matter of time until it returns. It's just like that cat that used to live across the street in the town where they'd lived before, when Chance was a little kid. Every time Chance went outside, it streaked toward her, scratching her ankles and biting. She has a couple of nasty scars to prove it.

Numbly, she begins to dress. She feels the two dominoes in the pocket of her jeans, rubbing against her hip, and ignores them. For now.

Her father has arranged for more days off, staying home from work so that Chance won't be alone. As if that will do any good. As if that will bring her friends back. As if that will erase what she has done. Or not done.

There's only one thing she can do to stop the pain and that's to keep her promise. She takes a deep breath and closes her eyes. This afternoon. She'll do it this afternoon. Chance opens her eyes and sees Mrs. Morin's notebook. It's green, her favorite color. She flips it open and, without really meaning to, picks up the pen. It's got green ink. She starts to write.

*Monday, October 16. Today will be a good day because it is going to be the end of the world. At least, the end of the world for Chance Devlin. Chance goes to school. She comes home. She tells her dad she is going to do homework, and then she climbs out the window and heads for the place. The place where they did it. By 5 PM it will all be over. The end.*

Chance reads the last lines a few times and feels a queasy kind of satisfaction. She hears her father's footsteps in the hallway and stuffs the journal into her top drawer beside the pile of notes. Then she follows her dad to the kitchen where she sees, unhappily, that he's made a big stack of pancakes.

She doesn't want to eat anything, but he looks so hopeful in his old barbecue apron that she takes a pancake, pours on maple syrup, and then carefully eats it, piece by piece. And then she has another. No use letting them all go to waste.

After breakfast, she grabs her knapsack and follows her dad out the door, stepping lightly around to his left side so she can hear him more easily. He doesn't have to walk her to school, as if she were a little kid again, but she kind of likes it.

Last year, when her dad had moved out, it had been hard. Really hard, getting used to all the empty spaces where he used to be. And since he's moved back, she can hear them sometimes, her mom and dad, arguing in their bedroom or going into the basement where they probably think she can't hear them. But he came back. And they told her they were going to try and make it work.

As they cross the edge of the yard, something catches Chance's eye from the line of pine trees that border the neighbor's property. A flash of red-gold. And a bushy tail with a white tip at the end. A fox? She turns toward it, but the animal—if it is an animal—is already gone.

"What?" asks her dad.

"Nothing," says Chance. "Thought I saw a fox. But maybe not."

"It could have been a fox," says her father. "Maybe that's your spirit animal, or animal totem, come to keep you company."

"Spirit animal? Animal totem?" asks Chance.

"Yeah. You know, some people think that animals can help us humans. Or that inside each of us are the gifts of a particular animal. Having the wisdom of a fox could be very useful. Following a fox could lead you out of tricky situations."

"Really?" asks Chance.

"Maybe," says her dad, his twinkly eyes smiling. "There's more to this life than anybody really knows for sure."

"I don't believe in fox magic," says Chance. Even a fox couldn't keep her safely out of reach of the Bad Thing. But for the rest of the way to school, nothing hisses at her heels as she walks along the sidewalk. And nothing stalks her across the school grounds, either. For the time being, she is safe.

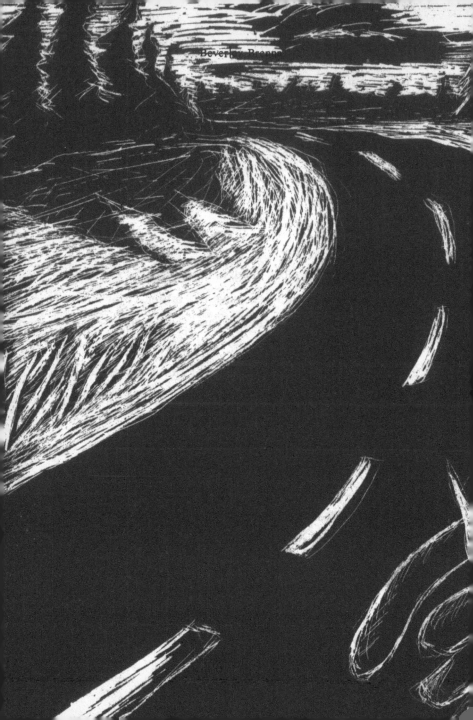
Beverly Brenna

# Chapter Four

Evading her father after school isn't as easy as Chance thought it would be.

"First, I'm going to help you with your homework, and then I'm going to stuff you with cupcakes, and then we're going to take a drive before supper," he announces when he meets her in front of the building.

"Cupcakes?" she asks.

"A new recipe. There's sweet potatoes in them. Not sure if I like them, but you can pass judgment."

"Sweet potatoes?"

"I got the recipe off the Internet. I was going to do a sweet potato casserole for supper, but cupcakes sounded better."

Chance shakes her head. It's just like her father to get sidetracked into a dessert recipe. He's got the biggest sweet tooth of anyone she knows. Except for Georgia.

Homework doesn't take long. It's just decimals, and Chance aced place-value years ago. Sitting beside her dad at the kitchen table, she's done in twenty minutes.

Chance is careful not to let today's collection of notes get out of her bag until she reaches her room, and then she puts them in the drawer with the rest. She reads them first, of course. She has to read them. She's expected them and she knows they are true.

Before the Bad Thing, notes like these really hurt. But now, when Chance remembers her disloyalty, the mean words feel deserved.

She stands by her dresser and explores with her tongue the last bit of cupcake that's stuck in a back tooth. They'd been surprisingly good. Without meaning to, she'd eaten three.

"It's okay," her dad had said, watching as she'd eyed the third one. "You're building back your strength. It's okay to do that, Chance. Be good to yourself."

So she'd eaten the cupcake, even though she disagreed with him. She shouldn't be good to herself. Nobody should be good to her, now.

The journal lies in her top drawer beside the notes. She brings it out and reads what she wrote earlier. Then she picks up the pen.

*Monday, October 16 again*, she scrawls. *Chance will keep her promise, just not today. Today she is pretending to be happy.* She thinks for a minute. Then she adds: *Well, mostly pretending. It wasn't as bad a day as yesterday.*

"Ready to go in five minutes?" her dad calls. "I'm just going to check the oil." She hears the door to the porch open and shut. Then she reaches into the drawer and pulls out one of the notes.

*Chance Devlin is a freek and a dyke. She should just die.*

Not much different from the other ones. She swallows. Probably it would have been better for everyone if she had died. Then her dad wouldn't be taking time off work and her mom wouldn't be taking those pills. Chance has seen the bottle on her mother's desk, pills to help her sleep. If Chance were dead, even the counselor would be better off—she'd have time for someone else, someone more important.

Chance looks back at the journal and writes: *But today was bad enough and it's not over yet. Tomorrow it's early dismissal and Chance will have time to do what she should have done in the first place.*

She thinks back to how it all started, three years ago. With friendship. She'd been a new kid here, most of the other Grade 4s already fixed up in tight cliques clustered around cell phones. One recess, Desiree had come over with a little cloth bag.

"I'm Desiree," she'd said. "Wanna play?"

"Okay," Chance had answered. Desiree opened the bag and took out a set of dominoes. Chance had heard of them but never played. The ebony squares felt cool and interesting in her fingers.

"Loser," someone yelled at Desiree as they carefully set up the dominoes.

"Loser yourself!" Desiree retorted. Then Georgia had walked by to see what the fuss was about and offered them a piece of her chocolate bar. And poked at the dominoes.

"My grandma has a bunch of these," she said. "Whatchamadingles."

"Who are you?" asked Desiree.

"Promise you won't laugh," said Georgia.

"We promise," said Desiree, looking fiercely at Chance.

"Olivia Gorgonzola. But you can call me Georgia." She looked at both of them as if to make sure they'd heard her, and then she smiled. "I'll bring my grandma's dominoes tomorrow." And so the domino gaming had begun.

At first, the other kids picked mostly on Desiree, but soon the meanness overflowed to Chance and Georgia as well. The girls didn't care.

"As long as you have a friend," Chance's mom had said, often, "life is good." And Chance had a friend. She had two of them.

Over time, the taunting shifted from "Loser" to "Lesbian." At first, Chance didn't really know what "Lesbian" meant. She looked it up online but didn't think very much about it. Finally when a kid in Grade 5 said, "You're such a Lesbian," for the millionth time, Chance had responded, "So?"

Wrong answer. From that moment onward, the bullying had been fierce.

Chance doesn't know if she's a Lesbian or not. Or a dyke, which means the same thing. She doesn't feel anything special for girls, but she doesn't feel anything special for boys, either. All of the boys in her school—the Grade 7s and 8s in particular— are creeps. And anyway, now that she's older, she knows that there isn't anything wrong with being a Lesbian even if she is one. After all, Ellen DeGeneres is gay, and there isn't anything wrong with Ellen. Ellen's famous. Lots of other people are gay, too—she's read about them on the Net. Big deal.

Still, the other kids think differently. Every day, she's been getting notes in her desk. Sometimes in her backpack, if she leaves it out. Once, stuck to her chair with spearmint gum. She pulls another note out of the drawer and reads it.

Traitor. You're better off dead.

The words hit her like stones. Then she hears her father calling something. She has to go. Chance stuffs the notes and her journal back into the drawer and pushes it shut. With the awful words rattling around in her head, she puts on her shoes and runs out to the car. It doesn't matter where they're going, as long as it's away from here.

As they pull out of the driveway, she catches a glimpse of red-gold in the ditch across the road. The grass is longer there, even in its autumn state, and offers a bit more shelter than the flattened lawns. The car speeds up and, for a moment, Chance sees the fox. Darting from cover and running alongside, as if it's trying to keep up with them.

"There!" she calls. Her dad hits the brakes and takes a look, but the fox has already vanished.

"How does it do that!" she breathes. "Snap! It's invisible."

"The fox again?" says her dad. "Must be magic, I guess."

"What? Fox magic?" Chance says. "I don't think so."

"Seriously." Her dad's voice is soft. "Animals can remind us of what's important. The fox, for example. It's clever and resilient. It can help us look at others and not be deceived."

"Not be deceived," Chance repeats.

"We have to think for ourselves," says her father, rounding the corner onto Main Street. "Not let other people think for us."

"They didn't ..." Chance starts. "I wasn't ..." She can't go on. She promised she wouldn't talk about it—they all promised. Desiree, Georgia, and her. And she won't. She can't.

Her dad places a big warm hand on her wrist.

"It's okay," he says. "But if you have more that you want to talk about, I'm here. Whenever you need me."

Chance looks out the window, but instead of the fox this time it's the Bad Thing that's running alongside the car. Her eyes fill with tears.

"Can we go home?" she asks. "I just want to go home!"

"Soon," her father answers. "There's something I want to show you first."

They pull into the hospital parking lot and stop.

"But this is the hospital!" Chance cries. "You tricked me! I'm not going to see any more doctors!"

"Whoa ... hold your horses," says her father. "This won't take long, but I told your mother we'd come by and see her at work. Okay? We're just here to see your mother, not any doctors."

"We're just here to see Mom?" Chance repeats. "On the baby ward?"

"Yup. Now wipe your tears or you'll make everyone cry in here and, trust me, they're babies, so they'll already be crying!"

The glass is smudged from so many visitors, but Chance can clearly see her mother on the other side, shifting from crib to crib, checking on the tiny infants. From time to time, her mom stops and picks up a baby, cradles it against her chest, and walks with it for a few minutes before snuggling it back into its bassinet.

Chance watches how her mother pays attention to each baby. When there are too many tubes and wires for a baby to be picked up, her mother leans over, stroking it gently. Chance watches as her mother's mouth moves. She's probably singing to them.

Her mother sees them at the window and waves. Then she blows them each a kiss. Chance thinks her mother looks older than she used to. There are lines around her mouth and her eyes droop even when she smiles.

Some of the babies need machines to breathe, and others are attached to tubes for feeding or other things. Chance has seen this all before. She knows that while most of these babies will live, some will not.

After a while, Chance realizes her father is speaking to her.

"What?" she asks, trading places with him so that he's on her good side.

"This is where I first saw your mom," her father says.

"In the baby ward?"

"Yup. The neonatal unit. Of course I knew her; we were in the same year at university, getting our nursing degrees. But when I met her working in here, it was like I saw her for the first time."

"She told me that she always wanted to look after babies," Chance says. "Especially the sick ones."

They watch in silence for a minute.

"Has she ever talked about our journey as a family?" her dad asks, finally. "How hard it was to have a baby of our own?"

Chance shakes her head.

"You know we ... we lost three babies before we had you, honey. Miscarriages." Her dad's voice shakes a little bit and he steps closer to the glass, somehow gaining strength from what he sees on the other side. "And then ... we lost two after."

Chance feels her breath catch in her throat. Why hadn't her parents ever told her about this? But maybe it was just too sad.

"We'd planned for you to have brothers and sisters," her dad goes on. "But it just didn't work out that way."

*I'm sorry if I've been a disappointment*, Chance thinks, but the words stick in her throat and she says nothing.

Surprisingly, it's as if her dad can read her mind.

"You mean the world to us, Chance," he says. "Nothing could ever make us stop loving you. And your mom—see how she's filling in the gaps? When she wasn't able to have the big family she hoped for, she chose to give that extra love she has to these babies. People thought she might want to transfer into another department, get away from Pediatrics for a while, but she didn't."

Her dad looks at Chance and she feels his warm gaze on her face, kind of like sunshine. "Your mom's found a way to be happy. She's made a life for herself that works. Even around ... the bumps we've had in our relationship. I haven't always

43

been ... well, I'm not perfect. Nobody is. But ... whatever goes wrong, a person ... a person can always figure out a better way. A new path. We want you to know that, your mom and I. To think about it. And to see these babies. How they are fighting for ..."

*Blah, blah, blah,* thinks Chance. *More to think about.* "It's not just about *time!*" Chance blurts.

"What?" asks her father.

"It's not about how long they have. Just having a long life isn't worth it sometimes," says Chance.

Instead of answering, her dad pulls a Kleenex out of his pocket. But the Kleenex isn't for her.

"Sometimes when people die, people that we love," her father finally says, "it's hard ... it's hard to go on living. But that's exactly what we need to do."

Chance feels hollow. She is standing so close to her father that his sadness rises up around them like water. She'll soon be drowning in it. She quickly steps toward the window and watches her mom and the other two nurses. It seems like a happy place, even though, for some families, it'll be hard when their babies don't make it.

She looks at a young mother sitting on a chair beside the incubator where a very tiny baby lies anchored with tubes and wires. A boy, judging by the blue blanket. The mother can't pick up the baby because of his medical needs, but there's a space where her hand can fit inside the crib, and she's letting him hold onto her little finger. He's holding on as if his life depends on it. His eyelids are shut. Chance thinks they look like tiny mauve petals.

"Okay, maybe it is," Chance blurts. "Maybe time is important. I get it. I get the message, okay? Come on," she says, taking her dad's hand. "Let's go home."

Her dad doesn't answer.

Chance tries again. "Dad. Could we go? I'm kind of ... I'm kind of getting hungry again."

"You are?" her dad asks hopefully, his voice husky.

"Yeah. Fingers crossed there's something good to eat for supper, because I'd hate to think I'm going to be eating more of those same cupcakes!"

"Well, I ... I thought we'd just finish them off ... as an appetizer." Her dad gives a weak chuckle and his eyes crinkle up the way she loves. "I only made five dozen."

# Chapter Five

At bedtime, Chance is cozily tucked up in bed, a mug of cinnamon tea in her hands. When her father comes in to bring her another cupcake, she groans.

"You've got to be kidding!" she says. "No more!" But she takes it.

Then she hears the front door open and her mother's voice.

"Hello! Anybody home?"

"Just us chickens," calls her dad.

"Watch out!" Chance yells. "Dad's got cupcakes and he's not afraid to use them!"

"Feed a cold. Feed a fever. Feed whatever ails you," says her dad. "But tomorrow, we're going to get some exercise. That's important, too."

"Exercise?" Chance repeats.

"You'll see," he says darkly.

After he's gone out and her mother has hugged her goodnight, she puts the light back on and takes out the green notebook. Carefully opening it to the first page, she reads what she's already written, sticking on the last lines and reading them twice: *Tomorrow it's early dismissal and Chance will have time to do the job she should have done in the first place.*

She picks up the pen.

*But there's more than one way to skin a cat.*

The words that appear on the page surprise her. She wasn't planning to write that at all. It was as if the sentence wrote itself. It was something that Auntie often said when they asked a question about fixing the car. *There's more than one way to skin a cat.*

She thinks for a minute and then writes something else.

*We planned the Bad Thing together. It was going to be beautiful. We were all wearing our best clothes and Desiree brought flowers for our hair. Georgia was going to bring chocolates, too, but Desiree said that was stupid and a waste.*

She stops writing. The impossibility of everything wells up inside. What can she do now? If she doesn't do the thing they planned, what will become of her?

Bad words whisper and expand into loud voices that fill her brain. *Traitor.* She was a traitor. The three of them had planned something and she'd been a coward. She'd let them down and now they're gone. And she is here.

Chance shoves the notebook and pen back into the drawer and closes it tight. Looking out the window, she sees a big white flake tumbling down past the glass. And then another. Snow. It's snowing.

Winter was Georgia's favorite season. Chance knew she liked wearing big jackets and scarves so nobody would see how fat she was. Desiree hated winter because she was always cold, but she'd grudgingly go out with the other two if they begged. Once last winter, the three of them had built a campfire at the edge of the woods and roasted hot dogs. Chance remembered wolves howling in the distance that night, and the aching brightness of the northern lights. And the stars. A sky brimming with stars.

"But it's too soon for snow!" she mutters to herself, thinking of those tiny babies and how someone will have to drive them home from the hospital when they are ready, and she doesn't want it to be through a blizzard. Seeing them gave her the same feeling as that campfire sky. A good feeling.

She recalls the tiniest baby, holding onto his mother's finger, and wonders what it would be like to be a parent. Then she thinks of her own parents, losing all those babies. How many had her father said? Four? Five?

Sadness engulfs her like a rising flood. It's a sadness so big that when she falls down into it, there's no light or air or sound. And she is sinking, sinking fast. She must have cried out because, in a moment, she feels strong arms around her. Dad. And then Mom, both of them holding her and each other. Holding on as if their lives depend on it.

She's having a dream. A terrible dream. The big cat is here and she is pinned beneath its paws, her flesh torn to ribbons. She wakes with a start, her breath coming in painful gasps. She sees her parents lying across the end of the bed where they'd somehow gone to sleep after she woke up the first time. Her skin tingles and she feels her eyes strained and wide. Sleep has always been her refuge. But no longer. The Bad Thing followed her here. Now she isn't safe anywhere.

It's after midnight, according to the clock radio. She slips from the bed, careful not to waken her mom and dad, and stands in the small space by the window. Out in the yard, the red fox is loping around and around. She sees it by the light of the moon.

Maybe it's found the scent of something. She's drawn to the hunt, if it is a hunt, with an uncertain hope of victory for the fox. Survival. It's all about survival. As she watches, the fox grows more agitated. It moves right underneath her window and raises its eyes, looking directly at her. What does the fox want? What is it trying to tell her?

Its whiskers twitch and it tosses its head. Their eyes meet. She takes another deep breath and feels oxygen reach the corners of her lungs, places where there hasn't been much air for a long time. She breathes again. The fox turns and lopes out of the yard, and Chance slides back under the covers. *Breathing in. Breathing out.*

She thinks about the babies in the neonatal unit. Especially the tiniest one, the little boy. He's the size of a puppy. Probably he won't survive. She knows that, from reading about babies like him. But maybe, she thinks. Maybe he will. The good feeling comes back. Hope. It feels like hope.

She drifts in and out of sleep. Suddenly, she is wandering in the woods, collecting flowers. Glad that winter is over. As she walks along, she is careful not to crush the stems or bruise the delicate petals of the blossoms in her arms. All at once, she is walking on a wide path. And she has company. The fox is to her left, stepping gingerly alongside.

"Do you have a name?" she asks the fox.

It looks up, as if measuring her somehow.

"I do," answers the fox. She can hear it as clearly as if she'd spoken the words herself.

"Well, will you tell me?"

"Promise not to laugh."

She nods her head.

"I promise."

"Janet Johnson."

She feels like laughing, but she's promised.

"Oh," she says. "I'm Chance."

"I know."

"I didn't think you'd be a girl," she continues.

The fox looks slightly offended.

"Why? Not pretty enough?"

"No, I don't mean that at all," says Chance. "It's just that—in books—foxes are usually ... um ... male."

"Well, I'm not in a book," says Janet Johnson. "I never had much use for books."

"Really?" asks Chance. "Not even *Tuck Everlasting*? Or *Harry Potter*?"

"No," says Janet Johnson.

They travel in silence for a few minutes. Suddenly, Janet Johnson darts ahead, turning into a deeper part of the woods, but glancing back, as if expecting Chance to follow. She does.

Soon they come to a clearing where the flowers are especially beautiful. At the far side, where Janet Johnson seems to be going, there's a group of headstones. As Chance approaches, she sees that they are walking on graves. This is a cemetery. Randomly, she reads the names and details engraved in the stones at their feet.

*Bertha Andrews, beloved wife and mother.*

*Dr. Frances Kawacatoose, rest in peace.*

*Daniel Trainor, poet and friend.*

The last row, nearest the trees, has smaller graves. She can see how closely they fit together. Five names stand out clearly: *Katie Devlin. Ashton Devlin. Myles Devlin. Vance Devlin. Cy Devlin.*

*Katie, Ashton, Myles, Vance, and Cy.* Her siblings that never made it. She kneels and carefully places her flowers on the ground.

On the other side of the graveyard is another path. Janet Johnson leads Chance along it through the woods, and soon they reach the school.

"It's not too late," says Janet Johnson.

"I've been late before," Chance answers.

"Not today."

"Is this where some kind of natural disaster happens and I sound the alarm, saving everyone's life, even the principal's?" asks Chance.

"No."

"Is this where I suddenly become everyone's friend and win a popularity contest?" she asks.

"No," says Janet Johnson, sounding irritated.

"Because it doesn't matter. Nothing matters."

"Just go in and see for yourself," says Janet Johnson. "I'll keep you safe. I promise. And when you're done, I'll be right here, waiting."

# Chapter Six

Chance walks slowly into the school. It smells as if the caretakers have just finished the floors and she sneezes at the pungent combo of wax and soap. She's never gotten here this early. Usually she's racing in just after the bell.

There's no one at the front desk. That's odd. There's no one in the principal's office, either. She walks down the gleaming hallway and into her classroom. No one is there. She stares at her reflection in the mirror the teacher keeps on the wall by the coat hooks. Her hair seems even more reddish in this light. And she's a lot smaller than she remembers looking.

Chance thinks for a moment of going back to the front door. It's kind of creepy being in the school when no one else is here. She must be incredibly early.

The desks are in pods, five students to a group. Chance navigates through the open spaces until she reaches her area, and sits down. She realizes right away that this isn't her desk. Her knees bump against the bottom. The pods seem to have shifted, and she's picked the wrong spot. As she gets up, something drifts onto the floor. A piece of paper. She reaches over to pick it up and freezes.

Your not wanted hear, you Asshole.

The note is written in the same black marker as the others. And the desk is full of them. Full of these notes, crammed right to the top.

*Who sits here?* Chance thinks. She tries to remember who's in this pod, but her brain won't focus. She starts to put the note back but that doesn't feel right. Instead, she pulls out all of the papers and spreads them on the table top. She's sure they are meant for her. They're just like all the rest.

She gathers them into one big handful and rises to leave, but something feels wrong. She looks around and suddenly has an idea. It doesn't take much—a few minutes and some push pins— and she's finished. Her arms are aching from the effort, but she feels much lighter as she walks back down the empty hallway to the front door, where Janet Johnson is waiting for her.

"All done?" Janet Johnson looks at her expectantly.

"Yeah," says Chance. "I guess so."

"Now what?" asks the fox.

"What do you mean?" replies Chance. "Don't you know? Aren't you supposed to be leading me?"

The fox smiles.

"That's not how it works," says Janet Johnson.

Chance looks at the fox and it's as if she were leaning over a pond. Or a mirror. Dizzily, she closes her eyes, and when she opens them again, she's standing in her room by the window, her parents sleeping on the bed. The room is dark and she feels sleepy. She carefully climbs under the covers.

Beverley Brenna

# Chapter Seven

When Chance wakes up, she is alone. She turns over in bed and smells something. Probably more pancakes. She dresses and goes into the bathroom. When she's done in there, she hears her father singing along with the radio. "There's no time to lose," he sings.

It's a song she remembers. An old song. Georgia used to play it on her iPad in the garage, while they were working on the car. Remembering, Chance freezes, afraid. But surprisingly, the Bad Thing isn't waiting to pounce. It doesn't seem to be around at all.

Her dad pokes his head into the hallway.

"Hey, there, *Ruby Tuesday*. Breakfast is ready!"

Chance takes a careful step forward and nothing bites. She takes another step and the way is clear. She goes into the kitchen and sits down at the table. It isn't pancakes. It's waffles. A big pile of them. Her father has also made whipped cream and the frozen strawberries in syrup that Chance has always loved.

"I'm not too hungry," she says, and her father smiles at her.

"That's okay. Just try a bite or two and see how you feel."

He is wearing the barbecue apron again. It's speckled all over with waffle batter. She feels sad when she thinks of him making all this food, and now she doesn't want any. She closes her eyes.

"Did you see the snow?" he goes on. "I found your winter coat downstairs but I couldn't find your boots. After breakfast, maybe you could have a look." She just nods. The thing she doesn't want to talk about is making a lump in her throat and it's hard to breathe.

"How about some chocolate milk? Or orange juice?" asks her dad.

The thought of chocolate milk makes Chance want to throw up. She takes the pitcher of orange juice and pours, her hands shaking. The orange juice is surprisingly good and the lump in her throat gets smaller. She takes a grateful breath of air and then drinks a little more juice.

"Freshly squeezed!" her father says.

When she finishes drinking, she has a couple of spoonfuls of strawberries and then goes searching for her winter boots while her father warms up the car. She remembers that the boots are in a box in the basement, and when she digs around for them, she sees something else. The toque that Desiree gave her in July, when Chance turned twelve.

"A winter hat in summer?" Chance had laughed. And it was the ugliest thing imaginable. Green and yellow, blue and red, with a big purple pompom.

"Just think," whispered Desiree. "You'll never have to wear it! But you could put a note inside, leaving it to someone you hate and telling them why."

The three of them laughed about it then. Chance isn't laughing now. She stands, looking at the ugly toque, and what she feels, flooding through her whole body, is confusion. Why would they have felt so superior, just because they had that stupid plan? And why would they have wanted to make other people miserable by giving them ugly gifts and notes?

She pulls out the note she'd written and left inside the toque:

Whoever finds this is as stupid and ugly as this hat.

She leans into the box and pulls out her boots, and then she tucks the hat into her coat pocket. Good thing her parents hadn't found it. As she walks through the kitchen to the back door, she pushes the crumpled note into the garbage, where no one else will read it. She remembers writing it. She remembers feeling angry at her parents for ... a bunch of things. But angry as she

67

was, no one should have to find a note like this one. Especially if she'd already ...

The snow has stopped falling, and when she goes outside into the freshness of the day, she tilts her head to breathe the clean smell of winter. Then she takes a few steps into the backyard, making tracks. That's when she sees the other tracks.

One line of prints is from Janet Johnson, she's sure of it. No one could mistake the fox pattern. Four pads with claws and a V in the middle. But the other set of tracks is larger, harder to identify.

She looks closer as the winter sun rises mauve in the eastern sky. By its thin, hopeful light, she identifies the second set of tracks. Definitely lynx, with its wide snowshoe feet. The two sets of tracks run around in a wide circle and then out of the yard. As if one animal were chasing the other.

At school, she is late again, and when she picks up the late slip from the secretary, Chance says, "Thank you."

"You're welcome," answers Ms. Whitefish, smiling. Chance admires her long dark hair and how it looks against the red sweater the secretary is wearing. Suddenly the world seems full of color again.

"Have a great day," says Ms. Whitefish.

"I'll ... I'll try," Chance answers, turning toward her classroom. When she opens the door, a big debate is going on, with the teacher looking around, trying to make sure everyone has space to talk. Chance sets the late slip on the teacher's desk and slides into her own seat.

"It's not fair," Dannika is saying. "Why do we all have to read that stuff?"

"Maybe it's better that we all read it, since we know about it," Danny retorts. "That *stuff* is everyone's problem."

Chance looks around to see what they're talking about and spots the bulletin board. It's full of the notes, the awful ones, pinned there right where she left them. Except she'd just been dreaming when that happened, hadn't she? But the notes are really here. And she knows they were written to her. Even though she'd found them in that other desk, they are definitely meant for her.

But someone's added new ones. Lots of new ones, fastened around the edges and taped onto the rest of the wall. And they're all horrible. She starts to feel sick. Do all the kids hate her?

"I don't feel as bad, now that I'm rid of mine." The words are so quiet that Chance can hardly hear, and she turns to a desk nearby where the new boy—a boy who arrived a few weeks ago—is sitting. He's a smaller kid and his skin is so blotchy that it looks as if he's sick with something. "It's when I read them, just to myself, that I start believing ... I start believing what they say," he says.

Chance sits up a little straighter. What is he talking about? These notes? Were some of them written to him? She looks inside her own desk. Two more notes are in there. She thinks for a moment and then stands up. But another kid beats her to it. Sasha has three notes in her hand, and she posts all of them.

Then it's Chance's turn. When she tapes hers to the wall beside the others, a few kids look away. She lifts her chin.

"They make me feel bad, too," she says. "And I'm going to leave them here. On this wall of sadness."

Monika rolls her eyes, but Chance looks at her and doesn't look away.

"Nobody should have to read these," Chance says. "But Danny's right. They are everybody's problem."

By the time the discussion is over, the sadness wall is full from one end to the other. *It's painful to look at, but good, too,* Chance thinks. *Kind of a relief.* They've decided to leave them posted so everyone can see.

"To help us heal," says the teacher. Chance looks at Mrs. Penikett, as if for the first time. The teacher's eyes are puffy, with dark circles underneath.

"I love you kids, you know that?" Mrs. Penikett tells them. "You know that, right? I love all of you."

She's said it before, but Chance hasn't really thought about it until now. Their teacher really does care about them. And maybe she's been really sad. Losing two students. Kind of like losing your own children.

Chance remembers seeing Mrs. Penikett at the memorial service. Everyone had been there. Mrs. Penikett was sitting with the families, and once, when she turned around, Chance had seen her crying. Chance had touched her own face, surprised to find it dry. Somehow she felt too awful even to cry.

And now it's time to move on. Mrs. Penikett is asking them to take out their notebooks and think again about the poem the class has been studying. It's a poem by Robert Frost called "Mending Wall." Chance hasn't paid much attention to it, but now she looks at the lines again. Lots of it she doesn't understand, but some of it she does.

"*Something there is that doesn't love a wall,*" she reads aloud. Then she puts up her hand.

"Mrs. Penikett, do you think we could put this first line back there? On the sadness wall? Maybe it would be good for people to know that we don't really ... that we don't really want a wall like this?"

The teacher looks at her for a moment and nods, considering.

"What do the rest of you think?" Mrs. Penikett asks the class. "Good idea?"

Some of the kids agree and some keep silent.

So while the other students respond to questions in their

notebooks, Chance prints out the sentence in large letters on a sheet of cardboard. Then she fastens it to the middle of the bulletin board. She doesn't understand some of the rest of the poem, but this line makes total sense.

"Mrs. Penikett, instead of finishing the questions, can I make a drawing to match the words that Chance has put up there?" It's Carlyle, one of the quietest kids in the class. Chance doesn't think she's ever heard him speak before. Well, maybe in gym.

"Good idea?" Mrs. Penikett asks the rest of them.

"Good idea," a number of the kids echo back.

"*He just wants to get out of work,*" whispers Xander. But when Chance sees the drawing, she's impressed. Carlyle has done a good job. It's an image of a couple of kids on one side of a wall and a bunch of kids on the other. On both sides, the kids look unhappy. Positioned in the middle of the bulletin board, it kind of becomes a mirror for what the ugly notes have done.

Chance reads through the rest of the poem. There are still parts she doesn't understand. And parts she does.

"*He is all pine and I am apple orchard,*" Chance repeats. It's one of her favorite lines. She likes the sound of the words and the way they make her feel. As if difference, any kind of difference, is okay. She thinks about asking if she can post these words on the wall, too, but stops herself. Maybe it's a dumb idea.

# Chapter Eight

The school day ends early because of a staff meeting. Chance's dad is waiting for her in the car.

"Can we just go home today?" Chance sighs.

"What about my exercise?" her father says. "I'm turning into a couch potato! Let's just take an hour for something healthy, okay?"

Chance shrugs. Might as well go along with it. Easier than arguing.

They drive to the bowling alley and her dad stops the car.

"Bowling?" says Chance.

"Might be fun," grins her dad. "My inner bowler has been striking to get out."

Chance shakes her head at his bad pun but opens her door. Might as well get this over with.

"Did you know that the earliest form of bowling dates to

ancient Egypt, over five thousand years ago?" her dad asks. "Then Edward III banned it from England so his troops would practice more archery, but Henry VIII brought it back."

Chance just shrugs again.

Inside the bowling alley, it's all lights and music. Rock videos are playing on screens at the front, and spotlights dapple and dance along the wooden floor. Chance slips into the bathroom for a moment while her dad gets the bowling shoes. When she comes out, he's looking for her.

"What?" she says. It's too loud in here to make out what he's saying. He's asking something but she just can't hear.

"Just *the toilet*," she snaps, and takes her shoes.

He gives her a strange look but writes something down on a piece of paper. When they get to their seats, she can see that the girl at the counter has already entered their bowling names on the screen above their lane. *Forrest Gump*. And *The Toilet*.

"What did you tell them that for?" Chance yells. "That's dumb!"

"Well, it's what you said," her father answers. "I didn't know. When we used to come bowling all the time, you always wanted to be Poop Dog or Baby Dipes. I thought you were just, you know, following tradition."

She shakes her head. That was years ago. She remembers that her father always had a couple of empty beer bottles lined up after those games. And then more beer would come out at home. But there's no beer on the table now.

"And Forrest Gump?" she asks.

"I like that movie," her father says. "And as Forrest said, *Life is like a box of chocolates. You never know what you're gonna get.*"

Chance thinks about Georgia and the treats she always carried in her pockets. Prettily wrapped Saskatoon Berry chocolates, and big round Rogers' Coffee Creams.

Her father is talking but she can't hear.

"Never mind. Let's just play!" she says.

At first, Chance isn't very good, but after a few tries she begins to get the hang of it. She's grown since the last time they went bowling, and now she can control the ball much better. Before long, *The Toilet* is beating *Forrest Gump* 180 to 125.

"No fair," yells her dad. "You're younger than me."

He winds up for a spectacular last throw, and somehow his shoes slip on the waxy floor and he ends up on the ground.

"Dad?" says Chance. "Are you okay!"

"Not sure," he groans, rolling around in the lane. "I think I've broken something but I'm not sure what."

"Your arm?" says Chance. "Your leg?"

Her father gets to his feet, looking disheveled. "Nope," he says. "Just my pride. Play again?"

Without really meaning to, Chance agrees. And according to the electronic score, *The Toilet* triumphs once again, this time

195 to 110. As they leave the bowling alley, Chance feels light, as if anything is possible. Something is flickering inside her chest that she hasn't felt in a long time.

As she gets into the car, she sees someone walking across the street. It's Georgia's Auntie Verdine. She's carrying a grocery bag in one hand, and a cane in the other, head down against the wind. Chance drops quickly into her seat. Suddenly, the little flame of joy is gone.

The last time she saw Auntie Verdine, a couple of weeks after the Bad Thing happened, she came over and practically begged Chance to keep working on the car. "Anytime," she pleaded. "Come on over."

But Chance can't imagine working on the Mustang. Not now. Not anytime. Thinking about that car sitting in the dusty garage makes Chance feel more desolate than ever before. She shouldn't be happy now. She should never be happy again.

Beverley Brenna

# Chapter Nine

On Wednesday when Chance goes into the classroom, she sees that someone has taped another picture onto the bulletin board. It covers some of the notes.

"Serena has brought a picture of the Métis flag," says Mrs. Penikett. "She wants us to think about how it uses the infinity symbol to represent the relationship of two cultures. Serena, can you talk about this?"

Serena looks a little nervous but she starts to talk. She explains how her flag holds people together.

"Maybe we need more things here to hold us together," she says. "Things that connect to our cultures. And remind us that we should treat each other nice."

"I've got an idea," Danny says. "Why don't we add other stuff to this wall? We can't take down the notes because we shouldn't forget about them. But we can move past them!"

Most of the other students agree.

"It'll be a *real* mending wall," says Raoul.

"That's not what the title of that poem means," snaps Monika. "'Mending Wall.' Those guys were just fixing a wall."

"And maybe we can fix this one," says Danny.

Mrs. Penikett slowly nods.

"I hope we can," she says.

Chance looks at Monika, who looks the other way. Then she looks at Raoul, who smiles. *Just one friend*, her mother would say. *That's all you need.* Chance starts to smile, but then she gets that sinking feeling again and closes her eyes. Just when things start going better, she's drowning.

The next day, Danny brings some photos from home. "I'm a Dënë person," he says. "*Dënësułnë*, my dad calls it. And these pictures show me fishing with my dad and setting a rabbit snare. We fish and hunt for food and we don't waste anything. We are respectful of all people and animals. Just like all of us in this classroom should be respectful of each other."

He pins the photos onto the wall, covering some of the ugly notes.

"And we should be respectful of ourselves. We are all ... worth caring about."

Mrs. Penikett smiles at him. "Everyone okay with these

pictures going on our wall?" Most of the kids agree, although Chance sees Monika scratching something into her desk, and Xander kind of smirking as if it's all too dumb to take seriously.

The day after that, other students bring more things to pin on the wall. Shelley brings a picture of a group of people baking something. "Lefse day," she says. "We're working together."

Donovan brings a picture of loaves and fishes from a story in the Bible. "It's about sharing," he says as he puts it up. "And hope."

Sasha tapes a photograph of her family onto the wall. "Love," she says.

And Dannika brings a plaque her grandfather has made, with the letters carved in wood. "*Wâhkotowin*," she reads. "That's a Cree word. It means kinship." She takes a deep breath and then she goes on.

"Kinship with all of our relatives. Even rocks and trees. Because we are connected with all living things, we're never really alone. We're never without family."

It takes a lot of pins, but Dannika finally manages to hang up the plaque with all the other stuff on the mending wall.

"*Wâhkotowin*," Chance says to herself, liking the sound of the word and the idea of being connected to everything.

By Friday, the wall is almost completely covered. "Can we take down the world map on the other wall?" Pansy asks. "So we have more room?"

"We can work around it!" Guy says. "That map is kind of important."

"Tell us what you mean, Guy," says Mrs. Penikett. "Why is the map important?"

"It helps us remember there's other places besides here," says Guy. "Other places that might be hurting. Other places that might need ... a mending wall, too."

"Hey, he's right!" calls Alyssa, a quiet girl who rarely says anything. "He's right! Can we put our mending wall on the Internet? That way we could send it everywhere!"

Immediately the students all begin to talk. A few of them say it might be hard work, and Xander starts smirking again, but in the end, lots of them agree. It's a good idea.

"I'll take photos of the wall with my phone!" shouts Sasha.

"I'll help!" calls Carlyle.

"What about ... what about all the bad stuff underneath?" asks Raoul. "Shouldn't we put that up there on the Internet? Shouldn't we put that up there as well?"

Monika suddenly stands up, grabs a washroom pass, and leaves the room, slamming the door. Mrs. Penikett slips out after her.

"No way! That all stays hidden!" says Dannika.

"Who made you the boss?" asks Pansy.

"Maybe I don't want all that bad stuff out there after all," mumbles Raoul.

But Chance isn't so sure. *It's not really a mending wall if you don't know what you're mending,* she thinks. But she doesn't say it.

Then another line from the poem comes back to her.

"*We wear our fingers rough with handling them.*"

She wonders what that line means. Maybe the two guys in the poem are wearing out their hands on the rough stones, fixing the wall. She suddenly thinks she understands.

"Maybe paying too much attention to the notes could wear us all out," she blurts. "We can't forget them, but we shouldn't waste any more time on them."

Then she drops her head, surprised at herself.

"That's a bit of a stretch," Danny says. "But I get it."

"Yeah," says Raoul. "It makes sense."

Just as the teacher comes back into the classroom, Carlyle starts to speak.

"There's still some places on the wall that need mending," he says. "Why don't we write nice notes to people, and then put some of those up?"

"I was thinking about that, too," says Mrs. Penikett. "In the rest of our time today, we could write down good things. Affirmations that show the kinds of things we want people to hear. Then if anyone wishes to include those on our wall, feel free." She writes a few examples on the whiteboard as Monika slams back into the classroom, looking like a thundercloud.

You are an amazing human being with lots of gifts.
Thank you for being part of this community. I value you.

Everybody gets out a sheet of loose-leaf paper and starts to write. Chance thinks for a minute. Then she prints her favorite line from the poem:

*"He is all pine and I am apple orchard."*

She thinks a little more, and then she adds:

*We are all unique. You are a good person. You are welcome here.*

The teacher collects the affirmations from everyone, shuffles them, and hands out one sheet of paper to each student. Chance unfolds hers and reads:

*Whatever you are going through today will one day seem minute. You are brave, you are strong, you are beautiful. Someone loves you! You are loved!*

For a moment her heart soars. Then she stuffs the paper into her desk. The person who wrote that doesn't know her. She isn't brave. She isn't strong. And she isn't beautiful.

Raoul stands up.

"I like mine a lot. I'm putting it on the wall so we can all read it."

He posts the affirmation and steps away. Chance sees her own printing. He's gotten hers. And he likes it!

> *"He is all pine and I am apple orchard."*
> *We are all unique. You are a good person.*
> *You are welcome here.*

Chance pulls out the affirmation she's shoved into her desk and reads it again. Then she stands up and pins it up on the wall, too, right beside *Wâhkotowin*, covering the note that says, "You're not wanted here." Someone wrote something nice on the paper she got. Why not let everyone read it?

When she sits down, she sees Mrs. Penikett smiling at her. Chance tries to smile back but her cheeks feel as if they are cracking open. She turns away.

"Oooh, Beautiful," whispers Xander, turning and staring at her. Chance ignores him.

After school, her dad is waiting for her, just as he's done all week. *Getting in shape*, he calls it. Chance thinks about how they've tried something every day, starting with bowling and then jogging, although the jogging didn't last very long. She wonders what they'll do today. Yesterday was hot yoga in the next town, and Chance wasn't sure her dad could get up off the floor after it was all over. He'd sure sweated a lot and his face was kind of purple. But he made it.

Now as she leaves the building, she shivers. The temperature seems to have fallen a lot during the day. She reaches into her pocket and then pulls on the colorful toque. Raoul is walking out behind her and she sees him look carefully at her head.

"Nice hat," he says. "Warm."

She eyes him suspiciously but he seems sincere. This toque could be a kind of test. Anybody who doesn't mind it might be worth knowing. *Maybe all the boys in Grade 7 aren't creeps after all*, she thinks. *Raoul isn't so bad. And some of the others, and the girls, too. Maybe some of them are okay.* The toque could be a kind of sorting hat, like in *Harry Potter*.

"I heard you were ... fixing a car," Raoul goes on. "I live right next door to her garage. I'm ... I'm pretty good with cars," he stammers.

"Maybe," says Chance. Then she thinks about the Mustang, and how it felt when she and her friends were working on it together. "And maybe not." She turns to go but catches sight of the look on his face.

"But if I decide to fix it some more," she amends, "you could help. I mean if you really want to ... and you've gotta know that there might be mice in there."

He grins. "Okay!" he says. "Okay!"

"How do you feel about driving Auntie Verdine around?" The words come out before Chance knows what she's saying.

"I would," he says. "It'd be fun. I think we'll ... we'll have it running in no time." She doesn't answer. A sudden image of Raoul and her in the front seat, with Auntie in the back, racing all around town while Auntie yells things out the window, makes her feel like smiling. But she doesn't.

Her dad is parked in the five-minute zone in front of the school.

"Are we going back to hot yoga?" she asks him as she climbs into the front seat.

"Never," he groans, rubbing his lower back. "Never. I have a new idea for today, if you're up for it."

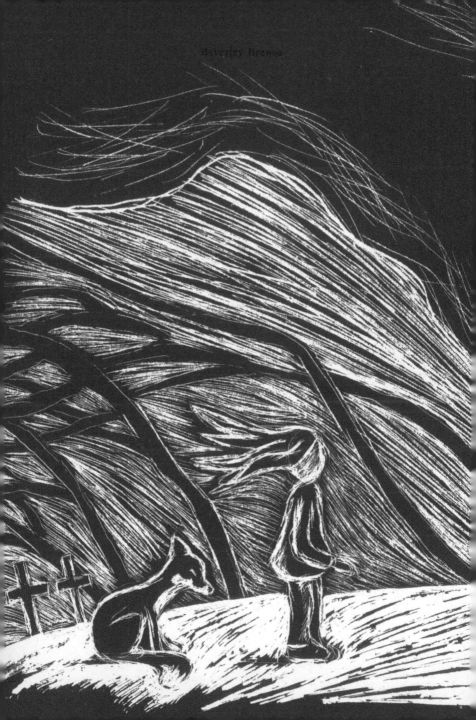

# Chapter Ten

As Chance sits beside her father in the car, thoughts and feelings tumble around in her head. For a moment, she wishes she had that green journal. She's been writing in it more and more, and it does help get things straight. The words come back to her now as if she'd just written them.

*We planned the Bad Thing together. It was going to be beautiful. We were all wearing our best clothes and Desiree brought flowers for our hair. Georgia was going to bring chocolates, too, but Desiree said that was stupid and a waste.*

*It happened on a Saturday. We went to this place we'd found in the woods. Kind of a clearing but with lots of trees all around. It was raining at first and I had on my blue jacket but then the rain stopped and I threw the jacket on the ground. I threw it right into the mud but I didn't care. I didn't care about that. Desiree's eyes were all puffy. I knew she'd been drinking.*

*And I knew she'd been crying but she said no. Georgia brought chocolate milk. I didn't bring anything.*

*We built a fire and burned stuff that we planned to get rid of, and then Georgia wanted to use the smoke for cleansing, but Desiree said there wasn't time. She said we had to hurry before anyone noticed we were gone and came looking.*

*I said, "What's the rush?" and she got mad and acted like I wasn't there, just giving orders and making Georgia do what she said. Just before it happened, I started to run. They were yelling at me and I just kept on running, and when I got home, I turned on the tv and acted like nothing was wrong. That's the part I can't tell anyone about. Running away on them and leaving them there. Leaving them there to do it without me.*

The car turns off the highway onto a side road and Chance stares out into the trees. She misses her friends but she's mad at them, too. Friends are supposed to keep you safe. Were Desiree and Georgia really her friends? And was she a friend to them? She sure didn't keep them safe. If anyone was a bad friend, it's her.

Soon her dad pulls off the side road and into a snowy parking lot where they stop. Ahead, the trees lean toward them, their branches piled with heavy snow. *As if they're trying to listen to us,* Chance thinks.

"Merry Christmas!" says her father, getting out of the car.

"Christmas? It's only October," Chance answers, following him to a man-made pile of fresh snow.

"Your gift is in there," he laughs, pointing.

"In here? Under the snow?" she asks, beginning to dig.

Soon she's uncovered them. Two sets of cross-country skis.

"From a garage sale," her dad says. "They're a little beat up, but I think they'll work. The boots and poles are in the trunk. I hope the boots fit!"

The last thing Chance wants right now is to put on the ski boots, but her father is so eager that she can't help but pull off her other boots and try them on. A little big, but she'll grow into them. They snap easily onto the bindings and then she's sliding forward toward the path.

She remembers this feeling from last year's gym class when they'd skied around the schoolyard. Weightless. Free. The path is slick and very well groomed. *Someone's already been out here today,* she thinks, moving along a little faster.

The woods are quiet. No birds. No animals. Chance skims along, trying to keep her balance, and for a while her mind is quiet, too. Then she realizes that they are not far from the place. The place where ...

Does her father know? Does he know that she's been here before? She turns to look back at him and realizes that she's already skied far ahead. Even when she cranes her neck, her

99

father is nowhere to be seen.

"Dad?" she calls, putting her poles deep in the snow to keep from moving forward. "Dad?" Her feet tingle with the cold. She's been skiing longer than she thought.

There is no answer.

Chance starts to clamber off the trail to turn around, but out from behind a tree darts the fox.

"Why don't you go ahead a bit further and have a look," says Janet Johnson. Her paws are deep in snow at the side of the trail, and she picks up one paw, and then another, as if to warm them. "Why don't you just see?"

Chance looks into the hazel-gold eyes of the fox and shivers.

"Maybe it's not a good time ..." she begins.

"No time like the present," says Janet Johnson. "It's just up ahead. Come on."

The fox glides onto the trail and then lopes forward, with Chance following. Soon they reach the spot. Chance can tell by the ribbons tied to the trees, the way the families have marked it as a place of grief. She thought she'd feel sadder here, but she doesn't. She doesn't feel angry, either. She just feels ... it's hard to find a word for it. *Empty*, she thinks. *I feel empty.* And ashamed.

The fox is digging under the snow and, in a moment, Chance sees her old blue jacket, right where she'd left it when the rain stopped that day. Suddenly her eyes are full of tears and her shoulders are shaking.

"You should tell someone," says Janet Johnson. "Tell your dad. Tell your mom. Your doctor. Your counselor. Or the counselor at school. Tell someone. And if that doesn't help, tell someone else."

"I promised ... I promised not to tell," whispers Chance, and the sobs heave out of her as if they are tearing her chest apart.

"Some promises are meant to be broken," says Janet Johnson. "Trust me. I know."

"How do you know?" Chance says when she can find the words, her voice almost swallowed in the new snow that has started to fall and the wind that is swelling like the tide.

"Because I promised to keep you safe. And I can't do it alone."

Chance looks at the fox and sees that one of her ears has been bitten off. There is blood on the snow nearby, and bits of fur, and the place is full of tracks. Fox tracks, but another kind as well. There's been a fight here and it's not over. A fight between the fox and the Bad Thing. The terrible memory of that day is out here, waiting for her. Waiting for both of them. She has to face it, once and for all.

And suddenly, it is here. The wind rises, the snow falls in buckets from the shuddering trees, and Chance is caught in a flurry of anguish. Overhead, a branch crackles with the weight of the storm. The Bad Thing comes straight for her, its mouth in a raging snarl, but she doesn't buckle.

"I'm not afraid of you!" she yells. "It happened and I'm sorry. But I'm not afraid. And I'm going to tell. I'm going to tell everyone! I'm going to tell—" her breath is pulled from her throat and her lungs start to burn. "I'm going to tell my teacher! And my counselor! And—" she feels something strike the side of her head and sees the fallen branch, but keeps on, "—and I'm going to tell my mom! And the doctor!"

Something blurs the vision in her left eye and she brushes it, the sleeve of her winter coat coming away red. "And I'm going to tell my dad!"

The fury of the Bad Thing screams in her face, but Chance does not falter.

"So you can just go away because you can't hurt me!" she yells. "You're a mistake! A really bad mistake! And I'm sorry for you, but we can't take it back in time for all of us. Just for me. And I'm taking it back now! I'm taking it back for me because I can!"

And just as suddenly as it started, the assault stops and Chance is surprised to discover that she's still standing. She takes a careful breath and then another. Her heart stops pounding. The trees are leaning in, as if to reach out and support her.

"*We are never without family,*" she remembers Dannika saying. "*Wâhkotowin.*"

The surface of the snow's been blown clean. Chance's knees feel weak but she knows she'd better get back. Darkness is falling.

But where's the trail? Stiffly, Chance turns one way and then another, trying to see a path out of this place. But she cannot. Then, out of a drift comes Janet Johnson, solid and familiar as ever.

"Follow me," says Janet Johnson. "I remember the way."

Before Chance leaves, she reaches into her pocket and pulls out the two dominoes. Carefully digging them into the snow beside one of the trees, she solemnly says goodbye to Desiree. Goodbye to Georgia. Goodbye to their friendship, because it's over. Everything is over. But other things are beginning.

It seems a lot longer getting out of the woods than getting in. Chance's legs ache. She licks her dry lips and tries to keep up with Janet Johnson, who's moving rapidly, even for a fox. After a while, Chance hears a faint cry.

"Dad?" she calls. "Dad!"

"Chance?" His voice is quivery. As if he's in pain. She skies toward him as fast as she can.

# Chapter Eleven

When she reaches him, her father is lying helplessly on the ground, covered in snow. He waves a pole at her.

"Take the keys and use my cell phone," he says weakly. "It's in the car. I've really hurt myself here. It's my leg." His face is lined and gray. She can see his right leg splayed out at a nasty angle. The sight of it makes her sick to her stomach.

Chance scrambles back to the parking lot and phones 911. She brings the phone back to where her Dad lies in the snow, and listens to the operator. At the same time, she is putting the car blanket around him and offering sips from his water bottle.

The severity of his injury doesn't really set in until the ambulance arrives and the paramedics give him something for the pain, splint the leg, and then load him onto a stretcher. Then she begins to shake.

The knowledge that her father is getting old hits her hard. How he had trouble getting to his feet after yoga. How he slipped in the bowling alley. He's not the same as he was a few years ago. And now this. She's sure his leg is broken.

She looks beyond the ambulance at the sunset, a brilliant pink shining between the still, dark trees. Her father's not going to be around forever.

"Why did you go so far ahead!" he whispers as she climbs into the ambulance to sit beside him. "I called and called. Then I started to think you were gone for good!" He looks sharply at the side of her head.

"And you're bleeding!"

Chance's eyes fill with tears. "I'm—I'm okay," she begins. "It was just a branch. And I'm sorry, Dad. There was something I had to do, and I did it. Everything ... everything's going to be okay." She leans over and pats his shoulder. "Not perfect, I guess, but okay. I'll call Mom. And then later, sometime when you're feeling better ... I have something to tell you."

He reaches out and takes her hand.

"Okay," he says. "Good. Good for you, Chance. My darling daughter. Good for you. And then ... and then, next time, when my leg is better, we need to try scuba diving."

Joy bubbles up inside her and she doesn't try to stop it. Swept up in a kind of happy dizziness, she feels relieved and then serious. Calm and serious. Her father's not giving up. And neither will she. *There's no time to lose.*

In the lights of the ambulance, Chance sees Janet Johnson lurking behind a clump of trees. She gives a little wave as the ambulance accelerates and, as they pass the fox, she sees speckles of blood on the white snow. Then she thinks she hears a voice speaking to her as if from inside her own head.

"You haven't seen the last of me," the voice says.

"Good," Chance whispers. "Because that ear needs some attention."

"What?" asks the voice.

"That ear!"

"What?"

"Never mind," says Chance. And smiles.

# Acknowledgements

I am grateful, as always, to my amazing editor, Peter Carver—your insights and writing wisdom continue to teach me important lessons.

Thank you to Chris Scribe, Director of the Indian Teacher Education Program (ITEP), College of Education, University of Saskatchewan, for your advice and encouragement related to Indigenous content. Thanks as well to Julius Park of the Saskatchewan Indigenous Cultural Centre for information related to Dënë content, and to Norman Fleury, Special Lecturer, Curriculum Studies, College of Education, University of Saskatchewan, for expertise related to Métis content. A special thank you to Desarae Eashappie, First Nations University of Canada, for a wonderful writing experience as part of the 2017 Think Indigenous conference that led to my obtaining the anonymous affirmation that Chance receives in this story. And thank you also to Jamie Gegner, Advocate for Children and Youth, for your ideas and encouragement, including suggestions for non-profit organizations where author royalties will be directed. Gratitude to Dr. Tim Claypool for support regarding mental health topics related to this book and for the inspiring and educational Afterword. Thank you also to Dr. Audrey Kinzel for incisive suggestions related to the psychology of my characters. While I am indebted to these mentors for their ideas and enthusiasm, any errors I have made in the completion of this manuscript are most certainly my own.

Appreciation to the University of Saskatchewan and, in particular, the College of Education for recognition of the importance of artistic work and for the sabbatical that granted me the time to complete this project.

Thanks also to Miriam Körner for her evocative illustrations! I appreciate how they have captured this story!

And as always, a heartfelt thanks to Dwayne, my sons, and my extended family and friends for your everlasting love and support!

# Mending Wall

By Robert Frost, 1874 - 1963

Something there is that doesn't love a wall,

That sends the frozen-ground-swell under it,

And spills the upper boulders in the sun;

And makes gaps even two can pass abreast.

The work of hunters is another thing:

I have come after them and made repair

Where they have left not one stone on a stone,

But they would have the rabbit out of hiding,

To please the yelping dogs. The gaps I mean,

No one has seen them made or heard them made,

But at spring mending-time we find them there.

I let my neighbor know beyond the hill;

And on a day we meet to walk the line

And set the wall between us once again.

We keep the wall between us as we go.

To each the boulders that have fallen to each.

And some are loaves and some so nearly balls

We have to use a spell to make them balance:

"Stay where you are until our backs are turned!"

We wear our fingers rough with handling them.

Oh, just another kind of out-door game,

One on a side. It comes to little more:

There where it is we do not need the wall:

He is all pine and I am apple orchard.

My apple trees will never get across

And eat the cones under his pines, I tell him.

He only says, "Good fences make good neighbors."

Spring is the mischief in me, and I wonder

If I could put a notion in his head:

"*Why* do they make good neighbors? Isn't it

Where there are cows? But here there are no cows.

Before I built a wall I'd ask to know

What I was walling in or walling out,

And to whom I was like to give offence.

Something there is that doesn't love a wall,

That wants it down." I could say "Elves" to him,

But it's not elves exactly, and I'd rather

He said it for himself. I see him there

Bringing a stone grasped firmly by the top

In each hand, like an old-stone savage armed.
He moves in darkness as it seems to me,
Not of woods only and the shade of trees.
He will not go behind his father's saying,
And he likes having thought of it so well
He says again, "Good fences make good neighbors."

# Interview with Beverley Brenna

**Why was it important for you to write about the issue of suicide?**

Most of my writing begins with ideas about a character, but this book came about a little differently. I started with the topic of suicide, and then the characters and plot developed quickly from that starting point.

I live in Saskatchewan, Canada, and in the months before I began writing this book, our news reports were filled with stories of young people taking their own lives. As a writer and a teacher, I feel a huge responsibility to pay attention to the world around me, and to support children wherever I can. The sadness I felt at these news reports fueled my work. I think that books can make a difference. Books can help us talk about important subjects and together work on solutions to our problems.

What Chance learns in *Fox Magic* is that many people care

about her, even though she feels alone. The more she shares her thoughts and experiences, the closer she comes to feeling better. Through the work of doctors, counselors, teachers, and her family, as well as Chance's own efforts, she is able to take one step at a time toward healing. This is a message that benefits all of us—and reminds us that when we are hurting, it's important to tell someone.

**You have said that in writing this story, you have used the technique known as "Magic Realism." What does that mean when it comes to your creation of the fox named Janet Johnson?**

I really have to thank the red fox who came to me in my dreams as Chance's guide. Janet Johnson evolved into a protector that uses Chance's own skill set to combat grief and trauma. Thinking about the fox's wisdom helped me consider how Chance could grow in her ability to learn from the experiences she has in the story, developing in understanding and maturity. I also think that Janet Johnson helped me lighten the tone of the story, adding humor, which in turn supports readability.

The idea of a talking fox suggests the genre of animal fantasy. However the story does not really unfold as a fantasy would. Yet while much of the book is realistic, there are places where readers might say, "Okay, that would never happen in real life!" Because of this blend of the real and the unreal, the genre "magic realism" seems to be the best label for this kind of story. However, because the talking fox only speaks to Chance, and we see Chance herself described in similar terms to the fox, it's possible that the fox is actually just Chance, giving herself advice. As readers, we can decide for ourselves what we want to believe, but there is a delicate magic available in this story if we want to see it.

**Chance's community is one where Indigenous people live—including the children in her classroom. Why was it important to you to have her living in this mix of cultures?**

In Saskatchewan schools, children of many cultures work and play together. So, rather than merely treat the classroom in this story with a multicultural description, I thought it was important to specifically include First Nations and Metis belief statements within the classroom scenes.

In 2015, the Truth and Reconciliation Commission of Canada released its 94 Calls to Action; Sections 62 to 65 connect to education, and education for reconciliation. These Calls to Action made me wonder what Indigenous knowledge and perspectives would be helpful to children in this story. Reconciliation is a responsibility shared among all Canadians, Indigenous and non-Indigenous. I tried to create the classroom setting in *Fox Magic* as a microcosm of what we should strive for in Canadian schools and communities: understanding, empathy, and mutual respect, along with a particular inclusion of Indigenous ideas as reflective of the First Peoples of Canada.

**In one of the most important scenes in the story, the students in Chance's class discover that many of them have been receiving abusive notes from others in the class. Why do you think some young people feel the need to bully their classmates in this way?**

I think adults, as well as children, sometimes choose bullying when they feel powerless. Through bullying, people can feel empowered, even though it's a shadow of the kind of power that good leadership brings. In simple terms, by putting someone else down, we somehow make ourselves feel better. But it's a mean kind of better, and it destroys our own chances for happy, healthy relationships and joyful lives.

Our choices in behavior are limited by the strategies we know. If kids learn options for how they can act, they can replace negative behaviors with positive behaviors. I remember hearing about a research study where children who were encouraged in creativity demonstrated fewer playground problems because they could think of alternatives to hitting a person who made them angry. If adults merely punish kids, without any other kind of behavioral instruction, then we are simply teaching kids to punish others, which can feed the bullying cycle.

**Bullying of various kinds seems to have become a major concern in schools in the past decade or more. What do you think would be the most effective way of overcoming this serious problem?**

There are many programs available to help school leaders understand and treat bullying. Thinking about the three roles in bullying situations can be helpful; the bully, the victim, and the bystander all need to learn positive ways to act.

**Chance has a number of adults in her life who are supportive of her as she works her way through her grieving and guilt. This includes her parents, Auntie, her teacher, even the school secretary. Why is this kind of adult support so important to a young person dealing with the kinds of issues Chance faces?**

I know from teaching that teamwork is the best way to address challenging situations. Through a supportive team, children can find the individual help they need, and learn to help themselves and others. A message here to readers is that if one person can't help you with your troubles, keep searching for someone who can.

As an educator who works with children and people who teach children, I can't emphasize enough the importance of every single person involved with a child. I've had students who connect to the school's caretaker as a mentor and friend, students who relate to an Elder or senior we introduce through shared activities, and kids who gain confidence through the support of a music or art teacher, through drama, or sports. As a parent, I know that my own children have benefited greatly from people outside our immediate family, and that at various times in our lives, many of us need people other than our own parents to provide models and opportunities for growth. Safe and caring communities are important for everyone.

**Chance keeps a journal tracing her feelings through the days she is dealing with grief and guilt. How important do you think it is for young people facing such issues to write down their stories?**

There can be great relief in sharing a heavy story, allowing the weight of it to shift from our shoulders during the telling. Writing is one way of releasing such a burden. In Chance's case, writing helped. It might not help everyone who shares the kind of emotional pain Chance feels, but it's one strategy that is worth a try.

I experienced severe bullying at school in my Grade 8 year. The journals I kept during that time offered some relief, as did the activities I enjoyed outside of school that let me view life as a bigger place than school alone. While I would not wish others to experience the bullying that I did, I think that because of that year, I developed an inner strength that has lasted a lifetime. My experience being bullied, unhappy as it was, may have made me a better teacher.

## Why did you name your main character "Chance"?

Sometimes it takes me quite a while to settle on a name for a character. As I began to write *Fox Magic*, however, Chance came to me all at once as a petite girl with reddish hair who solidly owned this name. Later, as I thought about her name, I realized her parents might have seen her as a wonderful chance for them to raise a family, just as she herself has a chance to live while her two friends have chosen otherwise, and so the name is meaningful in the context of the story. And maybe, just maybe, reading about Chance might give readers helpful ideas for their own lives, offering them important chances and choices as well.

**Thank you, Bev, for your thoughtfulness and for this story.**

# Afterword by Tim Claypool

For Readers Who Are Struggling With Mental Health

**Remember that mental health is as important as physical health.**

Can you imagine not brushing your teeth for a week, a month, or even a year? Maybe that sounds like a good break from this task, but, in the long run, your teeth will suffer. Dental hygiene is similar to "mental hygiene." Just like not brushing leads to tooth decay and gum disease, not paying attention to your mental health has long-term negative results, too.

**When we take care of important tasks—like brushing our teeth or talking to someone about a problem—we are helping ourselves.**

When we talk about our problems, we often feel better, just as Chance does in the story when she finally decides to share her secret. Feeling good about ourselves, making and keeping good friends, and planning for a happy future are all positive goals.

**Being unhappy with ourselves, feeling like "nobody cares," and thinking that "nothing good will ever happen" can bring us down.**

And sometimes when we're down, it's hard to get up again. We all want to feel good about ourselves, our accomplishments, our friendships, and our families. But sometimes it's hard to keep our busy lives balanced and happy. Perfectionists might think it is possible to be happy every single moment.

**But real life means finding healthy ways to deal with both the ups and the downs. Even though we may want to take charge and be in control of our thoughts and actions, there are many circumstances that are beyond our control.**

Life can be quite complicated at times. Friends move, parents change jobs, or adult caregivers decide that separation or divorce is the answer for *their* problems. Some loved ones experience health challenges that are life threatening. These are just a few examples of situations that anyone can face on a daily basis.

If trying to "control your world" feels like a losing battle, it is possible that support from a friend or someone you trust is needed more than ever. Even when you think that being alone is the answer, if you are thinking about hurting yourself, then it's important to talk to someone.

**Some topics may seem taboo or next to impossible to talk about.**

Sometimes you may feel isolated and unable to share your thoughts and feelings with anyone. The worse you feel, the harder it might be to reach out for support. But even though it's difficult, reaching out is important. Remember what Chance says:

"... I'm going to tell. I'm going to tell everyone! I'm going to tell ... my teacher! And my counselor! And ... I'm going to tell my mom! And the doctor!"

**Try telling one person you trust. And if that doesn't work, try another person and keep trying until you find help. Asking for help is important, whether it be from a family member, a teacher or school guidance counselor, or someone else. The search for mental health—relief from particular stresses you may be suffering from— will sometimes take you to someone who is skilled at dealing with mental illness, such as a counselor or psychologist. Both mental and physical illness have**

solutions—and both can benefit from the help of a trained professional.

Helpful information for you or someone who cares about you may be found on the following websites:

*Canadian Websites*

The <u>Kids' Help Phone</u> is available in every part of Canada:

>> http://kidshelpphone.ca/Teens/home.aspx

Among other services, the <u>Canadian Resources for Suicide Prevention</u> provides a list of crisis centres in every province and two of the three territories:

>> http://suicideprevention.ca/need-help/

The <u>Canadian Mental Health Association</u> has resources for people who are dealing with depression and mental stress:

>> http://www.cmha.ca/mental_health/preventing-suicide/#.WMcoQfIuwVo

<u>Canada 211</u> is a primary source of information on government and community-based health and social services:

>> http://211.ca/

***American Websites:***

<u>The Teen Health and Wellness</u> site can direct you to a range of information on various issues important to teenagers:

>> http://www.teenhealthandwellness.com/


<u>The International Helpline</u> site includes phone numbers leading to various supports:

>> http://togetherweare-strong.tumblr.com/helpline


<u>The National Association for Mental Illness</u> (NAMI) site includes a section specially devoted to teenage mental health concerns:

>> https://www.nami.org/#

For Readers Who Have Friends Who Are Struggling

**You don't have to be a lifeguard to save a life.**
All you need to be is the kind of person who is willing to be aware and take action when you think it is needed.

If you had a friend like Chance, would you have noticed the changes that took place in her during the events described in *Fox Magic*?

Would you ask questions when her mood changed and she lost interest in her normal activities?

Would you tell someone if you were concerned that she might be thinking of harming herself?

**Being "aware" means listening to your gut feelings.**
If you know the person well, then you might notice significant changes in mood that persist over time. These mood swings can have an impact on your friend's thoughts and actions.

**If you're a caring friend but don't take some kind of action, you would be like a lifeguard who refuses to get wet.**
Recognizing that someone is drowning may lead to throwing her a life preserver. But if a person is panicking or already "under," then more concrete action is needed to help him.

Ignoring or discounting someone else's feelings, mood

changes, negative thoughts or actions is similar to what is called the "bystander effect" when it comes to bullying. The problem is likely to get worse if someone who is aware of the bully's actions chooses to stand aside and ignore them.

**Instead of ignoring how someone is feeling, it can help if we try to "walk in their shoes."**
We can attempt to understand what lies behind someone's thoughts or actions. A lack of empathy, or a failure to appreciate what is happening to victims of bullying, or what is happening to someone with mental health challenges, is a way of ignoring one of the most basic of human needs—the need we all have to connect with another human being.

**Feeling a sense of belonging gets to the root of who we are as individuals; it helps to explain why relationships are so important to keeping our lives healthy and productive.**
Not everyone who has a "down" day or week will end up being severely depressed. Not everyone who is "down" or depressed will think about self-harm as a way to escape or find release from anxiety and painful thoughts.

On the other hand, we can never be sure who will allow negative thoughts to develop into negative actions that, in turn, might have life-threatening consequences.

**A professional counselor may be needed to determine the severity of the mental health challenges that an individual is going through.**

Counselors will be able to detect clues that an untrained person may brush off as "teenage angst" or the "growing pains" commonly associated with adolescence.

Even though friends and family members are important lines of support for a person in distress, sometimes professional help may be needed that involves a risk assessment and action plan.

**Planned interventions often include family members and close friends to help ensure success.**

Everyone can play an important role in the healing and recovery process. The key is to understand and accept the nature of that role, trying to take positive actions in communicating to people who can help. The websites in the previous section might offer useful information. While you may not be the lifeguard who jumps into the deep end of a pool to bring the drowning victim to the surface, you can be on the sidelines assisting and supporting to help ensure that a life is saved and a tragedy is prevented.

In *Fox Magic*, Chance was so caught up in the plan with her friends that she was not able to help them. Now she is trying to help herself. If you were Chance and could go back in time to the beginning of the suicide pact, what might you do or say that could make a positive difference to both her and her friends?

*This afterword was prepared by Dr. Tim Claypool, Department Head and Associate Professor in the Department of Educational Psychology & Special Education, University of Saskatchewan in Saskatoon.*